Who's that Woman in my bed?

Crystal Joseph

Burkwood Media Group
P O Box 29448
Charlotte, NC 28229
www.burkwoodmedia.com

Printed in the United States of America

ISBN: 978-0-692-11056-0

I must give my heartfelt gratitude to the following:

My husband, Stephen Joseph, for always inspiring and encouraging me to pursue my gifts. You are a true gift from God to me. I love you!

To my dad, the late great Starling Gibson – I did it daddy. I wrote a book. Thank you for loving me to my purpose.

To my mom, Annie Gibson – words fail and tears arise when I think of how you continue to lead me through life's challenges. Forever an encourager and a lover of the Lord, I am greatly blessed to have you in my life. Love you ma.

To my church, Bethel Gospel Tabernacle Inc., where my gifts and talents were allowed to be honed and flourished – thank you!

To the rest of my family and friends (who are just like family), THANK YOU!

Who's that Woman in my bed?

Don't fool yourself into thinking that you are a listener when you are anything but, letting the Word go in one ear and out the other. Act on what you hear! Those who hear and don't act are like those who glance in the mirror, walk away, and two minutes later have no idea who they are, what they look like.

~James 1:22-24 (Message Bible)

Who's that Woman in my bed?

I'm starting with the man in the mirror

I'm asking him to change his ways

And no message could have been any clearer

If you wanna make the world a better place

Take a look at yourself and then make a change

~Michael Jackson and Siedah Garret

CHAPTER 1 – THE PROBLEM

"He's got one time … one time to say one thing wrong this morning and hand to God, I'm going to …"

Raising her recently French manicured 'hand to God' while carrying a white plastic basket filled with freshly cleaned laundry proved to be a mistake as some of the clothing fell on the floor causing Megan to stumble.

"The fricking frack." she yelled while trying to gain her balance. A slight reddish hue appeared just below the surface of her smooth milk chocolate complexion. Megan was angry.

"Lord, I know I need your help because this day hasn't even begun and already I'm very close to cursing." Still holding the basket, she stood surveying the mess that now littered her gleaming mahogany wood floor.

"Sometimes I just want to scream." Instead of screaming, she continued walking past the chocolate leather sofa and dumped the now near empty basket onto the matching love seat.

"I wash his clothes," she muttered on her way back to retrieve the fallen laundry. "Fix his dinner. Clean his house. Do him, even when there's no guarantee that I will get done."

After each sentence, she angrily snatched pieces of laundry off the floor. A few strands of her jet black, naturally curly hair escaped the ponytail holder and fell onto her face. Pushing them behind her ears, Megan walked back to the loveseat and dumped the clothes back into the basket. Sitting down, she grabbed a towel and continued talking to herself while folding it.

"Every day I wake up angry. Every single day. I can't keep living like this. Something's got to give. I just can't …"

The stairs creaked.

Megan closed her eyes. *Here he comes*, she thought. *Not one word and I mean it. Just go to work and leave me alone.*

Opening her eyes, she slammed the folded towel onto the loveseat and reached for another.

Jim stood just over six feet tall and, at the age of forty-one, still had a full head of black hair with just a hint of grey at the temples that accented his light coffee complexion quite well. He walked downstairs half dressed in his suit pants and carrying his shoes. His athletic build, due in large part to a vigorous daily workout routine, was now visible as the stark crisp white shirt he wore was unbuttoned exposing his flat abs. He walked straight into the living room and sat down in the recliner.

"The kids' winter break is almost over," he said placing his shoes on the floor. "Mom called. She and dad will put the kids on the plane Sunday morning. They're scheduled to arrive in the morning around ten, so you know what that means," he spread his arms wide and grinned, "these are our last two days of freedom."

Megan continued folding the laundry without acknowledging her husband's presence.

Jim, noting the silence, continued. "I have to say, it's been real quiet around here without them. I kind of miss them. It's amazing how a couple of preteens can liven up a household, huh?"

~Silence~

"Not going to work today sweetheart?"

Megan placed the next folded towel on top of the other. Without answering, she removed her son's t-shirt from the basket.

Jim tried again. "Hey, it's Friday so, why not, huh? We all need a break from the day-to-day. Playing hooky can be very therapeutic, especially when it results in a three-day weekend." He tried to make her laugh by wiggling his eyebrows.

She placed the folded t-shirt next to the towels on the loveseat, reached into the basket and removed two of Jim's black dress socks.

"Oh good, just what I need. Honey can you pass those socks to…" Before he could finish his sentence, she rolled the socks into a ball and threw them. They bounced off his head and landed in his hand.

"What the…?"

Jim looked at her incredulously as she removed a pair of her daughter's gym shorts from the basket and began folding them as if nothing happened.

He stood, tossed the socks onto the recliner, walked to the loveseat and sat down next to Megan, inadvertently sitting on the folded laundry.

Speaking to him for the first time this morning Megan screamed, "Really Jim? I mean, really? You had to sit on the clothes that were already folded? Are you that inconsiderate?" Without waiting for a response, she roughly pulled the laundry from under him.

As she pulled, Jim pushed them toward her causing some of the laundry to, once again, land on the floor. Megan stared at the floor, breathing like a bull. Quickly, Jim picked up and refolded everything then slowly handed them back to Megan. Snatching the laundry from his hands she shook then dumped them back into the basket.

"Come on Megan. Was that necessary? I refolded them for you. You didn't have to put them back … in … the …" Jim stopped as Megan glared at him, her nostrils flared. Closing his eyes, he pinched the bridge of his nose – a habit he displayed whenever he was under stress. "Sorry Mimi," he said using her nickname, "I didn't mean to mess up your hard work."

That's the problem, Megan thought, *you never mean to mess up anything – yet you always manage to do just that.*

Jim watched as she took another pair of her daughter's shorts out of the basket and began folding without responding to him. He pinched the bridge of his nose again.

"What's wrong Megan?"

"Nothing."

Frustrated, he sighed heavily. "I never know what to expect from you."

She froze holding the shorts in midair. Slowly she turned toward Jim. Though her lips trembled, she willed herself not to speak.

She hates me, he thought as he lowered his head not wanting to see the loathing in her eyes.

Megan continued to stare until she was sure he wouldn't speak anymore. Then, she turned her attention back to folding the shorts.

When Jim spoke again, his tone was quiet yet strong. "It's been nine months. Nine months. I've apologized over and over again."

Megan closed her eyes. *Lord, I asked You not to let this man rile me this morning, yet he continues to do just that. Are You listening to me at all?*

"I went to counseling with you and on my own" Jim continued oblivious to Megan's silent prayer. "I spoke to the Pastor at the church because you wanted me to. I told the kids, which ranks right up there with one of the hardest things I've ever had to do in my life, but I did it because you wanted me to."

Opening her eyes, Megan placed the folded shorts on top of the other clothes, reached into the basket for a blouse and began folding. She didn't utter a word.

Jim was now pleading. "I'm trying so hard to right the wrong that I've done. What else can I do? What else do you want from me?"

Megan held the blouse close to her heaving chest. She responded through clenched teeth. "I. Want. This. To. Never. Have. Happened." Throwing the blouse on the floor she stared into his eyes. "That's what I want from you."

Shame slammed into Jim's chest like a sledgehammer, but he refused to look away. With a voice filled with regret he quietly replied, "I want the same thing Megan. I really do." His eyes were glassy. "I was wrong. There is no excuse for what I did." He reached for her hands surprised when she didn't pull away. "I love you and I want our marriage to work and I'm willing to do whatever it takes to …"

Megan felt as if her head was going to explode. Pushing him away she stood and screamed, "Whatever it takes? Why didn't you think of that BEFORE you cheated on me, Jim?"

~Silence~

"I'm so sorry Megan."

"You certainly are," she mumbled while walking toward the kitchen, "you are one sorry son of your mother."

Jim watched as she walked away unaware as to how her swaying hips in those snug size ten jeans, even during a time such as this, still managed to arouse him. But then again, she'd been unaware of his desires for a long time.

"I can't change the past Megan. I wish I could because God knows I would do everything different."

"Ha. Now he remembers God." She opened the refrigerator to get a bottle of water. Closing the door, she walked back to the living room and placed the bottle on the small glass-topped table near the loveseat.

"I honestly don't know what to say to you anymore Megan. Sorry seems so - so inadequate - but it's all I've got. I don't know what else to do. I guess I'll just keep on apologizing like I've been doing every day for the past nine…"

Megan whirled around in a fury and hissed, "Do you think a mere nine months can erase the pain you've caused me?"

Realizing he was fighting a losing battle, Jim stood. At five feet, three inches tall Megan's head peaked just below Jim's shoulders. Though he was looking down at her, somehow, she managed to make him feel small.

"No Megan. I guess nine months is not enough time."

Hands on her hips she snorted. "Oh really? You guess not? Well, I know not."

Sidestepping her, he walked to the recliner, picked up his socks and shoes and went upstairs to finish dressing. When he was out of view, she sat and tried to compose herself.

Get a grip and calm your nerves, she thought reaching for the water. Opening it, she almost drank the entire sixteen ounces in one swallow. Her hand shook causing some of the water to spill onto the floor. What a mess. Megan couldn't figure out if she was thinking about the water or her marriage.

Reaching into the basket she pulled out a hand towel and wiped up the spill then placed the empty bottle, along with the wet towel, on the side table. She picked up the blouse she previously threw on the floor and began folding it.

Ten minutes later as Jim descended the stairs fully clothed in his dark blue suit, white shirt and light blue tie, he headed toward the foyer. He had every intention of leaving without speaking to her. After all, how much could he take?

Opening the hall closet he grabbed his black wool coat, put it on, picked up his briefcase and started for the front door. Abruptly, he stopped. *I can't leave like this.*

Putting his briefcase back down, he turned, walked back to Megan and knelt before her.

The kneeling surprised her so much until her heart leapt with a feeling close to desire. She fought hard to smolder those feelings and successfully replaced them with anger - all in a matter of seconds. Briefly her mother's words passed through her mind. *Be careful about smoldering those love embers because just when you want that fire to roar - it won't.*

Not heeding that little warning, she rolled her eyes and asked, "Now what?"

Jim swallowed hard before answering. "Whatever you may think, I am very sorry. I'm trying so hard to make up for all the pain I've caused you. I love you Megan. I love you and I love our family and I promise to do whatever it takes to earn your forgiveness but …," he looked away, "you're not making this easy."

Her heart literally stopped. When it resumed beating and she was able to think straight she leaned down and placed her right hand on her right leg, just below the knee, to stop her from kicking him. "Oh, so now this is my fault?"

Jim was shocked. "No. I didn't mean to say …"

"Get out."

Stunned Jim began to explain but thought better of it.

Angrily he stood looking directly into Megan's eyes. She maintained eye contact with him. Neither said a word. Slowly and rigidly, he turned and walked toward the front door. Picking up his bag he reached for the doorknob. He spoke with his back to her.

"Watch your words Megan. Make sure you are saying exactly what you mean." Megan stood. "Get out now."

Furious, he turned and walked back to Megan. "You know what, you are something else," he yelled. "You walk around here like I have to kiss your feet or something."

Megan smiled. "I never said that."

Jim ignored her response. "And the sad part is, I do it. I do it because I was wrong. I was wrong, I admit it and I owe you that much but listen and listen good, I won't tolerate you disrespecting me in MY house in front of MY children …"

"Your children?!" Megan screamed.

"Yes, my children. They're mine too and I won't tolerate – no, I can't tolerate much more of your attitude. So, when you speak to me, again I say, make sure you are saying EXACTLY what you mean."

Megan rose up on her tiptoes in an attempt to get in Jim's face. "Get. Out. Now." She lowered herself and folded her arms waiting for him to obey.

"You got it." Jim turned and left slamming the front door so hard the entire house shook.

Overcome with rage her hands trembled. She tried to resume her duties by sitting down to continue folding the laundry but, while reaching for a towel, she ended up overturning the entire basket.

Unable to stop herself, she ran to the front door and looked out the peephole. Jim's car was gone. She began screaming inside the now empty house.

"Why did you do this to me Jim?" she yelled. "You ruined my life. How can I trust you? How can I – how can I love you again? How can I forgive you for this? How? I can't – I can't forgive you. Not until - not unless - oh God."

Feeling the tears about to surface she swallowed hard. "I will not cry. He's not worth my tears."

Absently, she picked up the empty water bottle and walked to the kitchen putting it in the recycle bin. She went back, took the folded clothes off the loveseat, threw them in the basket along with the used wet hand towel and dumped the whole thing in the hall closet.

"Hiding my dirty laundry." She smiled though it never touched her eyes. "Something I do quite well now-a-days."

Closing the closet door, she looked at the diamond tennis bracelet style watch on her wrist. The matching earrings and necklace were upstairs inside the cherry wood jewelry armoire in the bedroom. All three were given to her after the incident. Once again, she smiled. "The incident," she said softly to herself while closing the closet door.

She reached for the phone, sliding down onto the floor as she dialed.

"Wanda? It's me. I don't want you to say a word. I don't want to have a conversation. I want to do all of the talking. I need to tell you something then I'm hanging up."

She paused. "Wanda?"

"I'm listening." Wanda responded.

Taking a deep breath, Megan continued. "I know you think I'm crazy but, I did it. I had too. Like I said, I don't want to have a conversation about this."

Megan paused again. "Are you still there?"

"Yes Megan. You told me not to say anything, right?"

"It's just that sometimes your cell drops calls so I'm checking, making sure I'm not talking to dead air."

"You sound like you've been crying."

"I don't want a conversation Wanda!" Megan yelled.

"Ok. Ok."

"I need to tell you what I'm about to do in case something happens."

"Now I'm getting nervous Megan. I'm coming over."

"NO!" Megan screamed. "Promise me you won't come over here. Go to work. I'm fine Wanda. Don't come here. Promise me. Please?"

Wanda paused before answering, "Ok. I won't come over, at least, not right now. That's the most I can promise you."

"That's good enough."

"I hope you know what you're doing Megan."

Megan took another deep breath, "I hope so too. I've got to go." Before hanging up she whispered, "Pray for me."

Pressing the 'end' button before her sister could respond, she placed the phone back on the charger, took one last look around and ran upstairs.

CHAPTER 2 – THE CONFRONTATION

Megan leaned against her bedroom door. The new California King bed they purchased nine months ago fit nicely with room to spare. The snow-white comforter she fought to get (Jim thought white was impractical because the children spent a lot of time in their room, but she'd won that argument, which really wasn't much of an argument now that she thought about it) looked beautiful lying across the bed. The brightly colored throw pillows added a nice touch.

Megan stepped inside, her feet sinking into the plush lavender carpet. She walked up to the full-length oval shaped mirror standing next to the cherry wood dresser and stared at herself.

"Get it together Mimi," she said to her reflection in the mirror. "Let's see," twisting from one side to the other she continued, "small waist – check. Breasts still somewhat perky with the help of a good bra - check. Not a bad booty for 40." Doing a 180, she turned her head to see her backside, which was now facing the mirror. "In fact, it's kind of magnificent if I do say so myself." She laughed.

"That's what Jim use to call it. Magnificent derrière – M.D. when he flirted with me. That was our little secret. I would sashay toward him in a crowded room. His eyes would darken with desire. When I got closer he would gently blow into my ear then whisper 'M.D.' and I would melt into his arms. Oh God, where did we go wrong?" Tears sprang into her eyes but again, she fought hard not to let them fall.

Taking a deep breath, she walked to the vanity in the master bathroom and sat down. Automatically, she reached for a wet facial wipe and washed her face. Then, reaching for the moisturizer, she gently massaged the rich cream over her forehead, eyes, cheeks, chin and lips.

Slowly she opened her makeup bag and removed the foundation. Using a makeup brush, she covered the small blemishes on her skin. After achieving the desired glow, she applied rose-colored blush to her cheeks, dark brown eyeliner and black mascara to her eyes and finished it off with plum lip-gloss. Rubbing her lips together she looked in the mirror.

"Hmmm." She smiled but as she continued staring little imperfections became apparent.

"Oh well. It is what it is." No matter how many people told her she was beautiful, and there were many, Megan always found it hard to believe.

The doorbell rang. She gripped the edge of the vanity. "God help me if I'm not crazy. God help us all if I am."

She stood and walked back to the full-length mirror in the bedroom. "Tight jeans, yellow form fitting t-shirt and beautifully polished toe nails – not bad if I do say so myself." Megan thought hard about her outfit for this meeting. She decided to go with casual yet form fitting to show off her shape. She vacillated between heels or flat shoes before finally settling on her bare feet. A few years earlier she was asked to become a foot model but was unable to accept the offer due to her other commitments. Since, then, she always finds an excuse to display them.

The doorbell chimed again, the sound causing an eerie calm to come over her. Turning, she walked out of the bedroom door and slowly down the stairs.

"Showtime".

~~~~~~~~~~

There are two frosted sidelights on the front door that illuminate the shape and size of the person outside. Though not clear enough for a positive identification, Megan knew exactly who it was, and that knowledge angered her. She opened the front door and literally turned
~~~~~~~~~~

and walked away without speaking or even acknowledging the presence of her visitor.

Alrighty then, Stephanie thought as she peered inside and watched Megan walk away. She jingled the car keys still in her hand. Maybe this wasn't such a good idea.

She started to leave but instead, threw the car keys inside her red leather tote bag and entered the house. "Guess she's leaving it up to me to close the door," she muttered under her breath while closing the front door.

"Showtime."

Briefly looking upward to whisper a silent prayer, she followed the path Megan took, the three-inch heels on her black and red leather pumps clicking against the hardwood floor. As she entered the living room she saw Megan half lying / half sitting on the loveseat drinking from a teacup.

Pretty, Stephanie thought staring at Megan whose hair was now pinned up with loose curls cascading down the sides of her face. *Thought she'd look old and tired but she is very pretty. Doesn't help.*

Megan stared at Stephanie who was dressed in a lavender pinstriped suit – the fitted jacket accentuating her small waist. The matching pencil skirt stopped just before her knee, showing a very impressive pair of shapely legs. The first three buttons on her jacket were undone, exposing a silk white V-neck shell that slightly revealed her cleavage in a sexy yet tasteful manner.

Pretty, Megan thought. *Young. Figures. Looks Spanish. Maybe Puerto Rican or Dominican. Then again, maybe not. Definitely uncomfortable though. Good.*

The thought of Stephanie being uncomfortable made Megan smile so to hide it, she picked up the empty teacup and sipped. Megan felt as though she would need a prop, something to hide her nervousness. Since she has a habit of wringing her hands when she's nervous, she thought of a teacup and quickly grabbed one to place on the side table just before she opened the door. Holding onto something will stop her anxious hand movements.

Stephanie remained standing.

Let's see how long you're going to stand there looking stupid because I'll die first before offering you a seat in my house.

It became obvious to Stephanie that she would not be offered a seat, so she took it upon herself to sit down in the recliner. The fact that it was previously occupied by Jim a few hours earlier did not escape Megan, who continued sipping the non-existing liquid from her cup.

Stephanie nervously tucked her shoulder length, bone straight, honey colored hair behind her right ear revealing a small diamond stud. *What if she has a knife or a gun tucked in the corner of that loveseat?* She thought. *Why did I agree to do this?*

Stephanie slipped her hand into her jacket pocket feeling for the switchblade her close friend Flo gave her yesterday specifically for this meeting. Flo said, "If I can't talk you out of this ridiculous idea of going to meet with this woman on her turf, then you bets believe I'm going to make sure you are armed. You better bring the extremely dangerous part."

Though Stephanie laughed at Flo she still took the knife. Now face to face with Megan, she was very glad she did. Knowing she had neither the inclination nor the heart to use it, she was still glad it was in her pocket. It's presence made her feel as though she wasn't alone. It made her feel like Flo was nearby.

But she's not, Stephanie thought and felt the first symptoms of a panic attack. Outwardly though, she looked calm.

It's obvious she's content with watching me. Trying to intimidate me. Probably hoping I'd get up and run. Well sorry to disappoint you lady. Taking another deep breath

Stephanie said, "I'm glad you called and ask for this meeting."

Megan sipped and watched.

"I'm not going to act as if I don't know the reason why you asked me here. You said you wanted to talk woman-to-woman which is why I agreed to this but, just so you know, I'm out of here the minute I sense trouble. We are both grown, intelligent women who should be able to have a decent, drama free conversation. I didn't come here for drama and I hope you didn't ask me to come here for that."

Megan continued sipping and watching.

Stephanie swallowed hard to stave off the panic. Trying desperately to control her breathing she asked, "Why did you ask me to come here if you're not going to talk to me?"

Megan put the cup down on the side table, away from Stephanie. No need for her to know it's empty. "I think a better question to ask is why did you come?"

"I came because you asked me to."

Megan smirked, "And I didn't even have to give you directions. Imagine that."

Stephanie pulled her bag closer. "I think I'd better leave. This wasn't such a good idea after all." She stood and turned to walk down the hall toward the front door.

"You ruined my life." It came out as a whisper. Megan could've slapped herself.

Stephanie heard the whispered statement and it broke her heart. She sat back down. Her own voice was just above a whisper. "I didn't mean too. I wasn't thinking about you."

"You ruined the lives of my children too." Her voice was stronger. Megan was relieved.

Stephanie bit her lip. *This is harder than I thought.* "I didn't mean to ruin the lives of your children. Like I said, I wasn't thinking about you or them at the time."

Megan could feel the rage building as she fought with every fiber of her being not to jump across the room and slap the woman. Feeling a need for her prop, she reached for the teacup, but her hand was trembling. Quickly she put it back down and firmly clasped her hands together hoping Stephanie didn't see the tremble and willing herself not to wring her hands showing her nervous 'tell'.

Megan continued, "Tell me something honey, the fact that you weren't thinking, is that supposed to make all of this better?"

Stephanie would not – could not - look at Megan. She whispered, "No. But it's the truth."

Megan laughed. It was a harsh, bitter laugh that stopped almost as abruptly as it began. Her next words were like whips cutting into Stephanie's flesh. "You slept with my husband."

And there it is. Well, it's either fight or flight, Stephanie thought as she stood.

"Sit down. I'm not finished yet."

For some reason, Stephanie obeyed, which shocked both of them. Stephanie continued looking at the floor, but she could feel Megan's eyes on her.

"Like I said, you slept with my husband. That makes you a liar and a cheat. You don't know what truth is."

She felt her hands taking on a life of their own. That 'willing' them not to wring was not working so she reached for the teacup but as she reached out, Megan accidentally knocked it over. It hit the floor with a thud and broke causing both women to look at the same time. Quickly it became quite apparent to Stephanie that nothing was ever in it. Both women looked at each other.

~Silence~

Stephanie was furious. "Did you ask me to come here just to humiliate me?" Stephanie hadn't meant to speak. She had every intention of exiting the premises but the words were out of her mouth before she could stop them.

Temper hit Megan so hard and so fast until, for a few seconds, she was dizzy. Her world literally spun around. Placing her feet on the floor she raised her body to a full sitting position. "I ought to beat the crap out of you right now."

Stephanie slipped her hand into her jacket pocket and wrapped it around the handle of the switchblade. She stood. "I shouldn't have come here."

Megan stood. "You are so right honey. You NEVER should've come here. You NEVER should've slept with MY husband and you NEVER should've been in MY bed." Her chest heaved as she screamed the last sentence. Her hands were fisted on her hips, her nails cutting into her palms.

Stephanie was afraid but fought hard not to show it. *I've got to get out of here, but I don't want to turn my back on this woman. Always keep your eyes on the enemy. Isn't that what Flo said?*

She looked at Megan, standing, staring and breathing like a grizzly bear. *Forget that, I've got to get out of here now before I can't.* She turned her back on Megan and quickly walked toward the front door. As her heels hit the floor, she heard Megan's footsteps following close behind.

Uh, huh. I'm not getting caught out here like this. Abruptly, she stopped and turned around in one motion. The move was so sudden Megan had to pull back so as not to run into her. They stood a foot apart. The force of Megan's breathing caused Stephanie's hair to flutter.

"Why are you stopping? Huh? Get out of here now and stay out you…"

"Wait!"

Megan's eyes widen in surprise. "Wait? Oh, so now you're giving me orders in my own house. Are you really that …"

Stephanie interrupted her again. "You asked me over here to talk woman-to-woman, right? So, here I am." She paused to control her emotions. "Woman-to-woman, he told me it was over." Stephanie tried to keep the tears out of her eyes as she steadied her voice.

Megan took a step back and folded her arms across her chest. She didn't say a word.

Stephanie continued, "He said he loves you. He said he never...," she paused. *Get it together girl. Don't cry. Not in front of this one.* "…he said he never loved me." Her head dropped. Suddenly, she was emotionally drained.

"Good."

Stephanie's head snapped up. "Good?"

Megan smiled.

Now Stephanie was furious. She tilted her head to the side. *I tried to be nice. Tried to do the right thing. Guess you have to deal with people the same way they deal with you.*

"Let me ask you a question."

Megan unfolded her arms. "What you mean to do is ASK me if you can ASK me a question. But, seeing how classless you are, I'll ignore your ignorance. Go ahead. Ask."

Stephanie continued, "After you found out about all of this, you didn't throw him out, did you?"

Megan leaned back and arched her expertly threaded eyebrow. "That's none of your business."

"You forgave him?"

The pounding in Megan's chest returned. "And?"

"And you're still together? Family still intact?"

Megan's hands were now by her sides balled into fists. "So?"

"So - you won."

"I what?" Megan stepped closer, her bare feet almost touching the tips of Stephanie's shoes. Stephanie did not back up but put her hand back inside her jacket pocket and gripped the handle of the switchblade.

"Did you just say I won?" Clenching and unclenching her fists she continued. "Every time he goes on a business trip, I will wonder." She folded her arms to keep from swinging them at her. "Every time he has to work late," she pointed at Stephanie, "I will wonder."

Unexpectedly overcome with sorrow, Megan could barely breathe. "Every time he touches me …" unable to finish instinctively she hugged herself, slowly moving her hands up and down her arms for comfort. When she looked at Stephanie, her eyes were glassy, filled with grief, despair and that ever present anger. "Is that what you call winning?"

There was a full minute of silence between the two ladies as each worked vigorously yet silently to control their own emotions.

Stephanie looked down the hall toward the living room and saw the large framed wedding picture hanging on the wall.

They look happy.

That realization broke her heart. Still looking at the picture she spoke more to herself than to Megan. "I thought we had something."

"Shut up."

Stephanie didn't hear her. It was almost as if she fell into a trance. "I thought he loved me."

"I said shut up."

Stephanie had to rip her eyes from the photo to look at Megan. "Don't you see? We didn't have anything. He never loved me. He never …," tears rolled down her face as reality hit her very hard, "… loved me."

Megan thought she was going insane because briefly – very briefly - she actually felt sorry for this woman.

Stephanie wiped the tears from her eyes. "You still have Jim."

It was the first time she said his name and the sound of it made Megan cringe.

Stephanie continued, "He'll come home to you every night. Every night, I go home to an empty home. To nothing. To no one."

Megan wanted to kill her. "Do you really think your tears matter to me? Stop your crying honey because nobody here cares."

She mimicked Stephanie, "I go home to an empty home. Boohoo."

Her voice returned to normal, "So now I'm

supposed to feel sorry for you? You stole something from me. Something that was mine – is mine. So, if you think I'm going to feel sorry for you then you're out of your ENTIRE mind."

I'm standing here crying in front of a lunatic, Stephanie thought. *I'm getting out of here. Very, very, very bad idea agreeing to this meeting.*

She turned quickly, walked to the front door and opened it but just before stepping out onto the porch, she turned to face Megan. "I'm woman enough to admit I was wrong. I knew he was married and, being a Christian, it did matter but …" she paused to get herself together. "Anyway, woman-to-woman, I'm sorry for what I did to you." Her eyes glistened again as she half whispered, "and to me."

Megan nearly lost her mind. "What kind of apology is that? Get out of my house. Stay away from my husband. Stay out of his life and mine. In fact, do me a favor – DROP DEAD!"

Stephanie stepped outside the door. Megan leaned out and lowered her voice. "Ever since I found out about 'all of this' as you so aptly put it, I've wondered. See, my husband is very - fertile. So, I must admit I'm grateful to God that you didn't have a - what would it be called - oh yes, a bastard."

Stephanie's eyes widened in shock. "What kind of a Christian are you?" Before Megan could respond Stephanie continued, "If this is how you act on a daily basis, then it's no wonder Jim turned to me."

"Why you little …" before she finished her sentence, Stephanie pulled the front door closed.

By the time Megan opened it, Stephanie was running to her car. Megan started to yell but looked across the street and saw her seventy-five-year-old neighbor Mrs. Templeton outside dressed in a long winter coat, sweeping her porch.

Megan smiled, waved and spoke under her breath. "The nosiest woman in the world had to be outside today of all days. That's all I need is for her to tell the neighborhood how I was screaming at that woman."

Mrs. Templeton waved back but stopped sweeping and turned to look as Stephanie's car sped off the block. She looked back at Megan.

"Take care Mrs. Templeton and have a good day you nosy bat." She whispered the last part.

"You too Megan." Mrs. Templeton replied.

Megan kept the smile plastered on her face until she closed the door, then she slid down onto the floor in utter misery.

CHAPTER 3 – MI FAMILIA

Thirty seconds later, the doorbell rang.

Megan stood. "No that hussy didn't come back here," she said to herself. "Well Mrs. Templeton, I'm about to give you something to gossip about because if she has the audacity to come back to my house, we're going to throw down right on the front steps."

She whipped open the door to find her sister Wanda standing outside. Megan was confused. "What are you doing here?"

"After talking to you this morning, I went to the office but couldn't concentrate so I told my assistant to call if I'm needed. I left the office and drove across town to be here with you."

As her sister spoke, Megan leaned against the door and stared at the sky. It was so bright. So blue. Cloudless.

So – perfect. So opposite from the horror going on in her life.

"Can I come in?"

Megan stepped aside. Wanda walked inside.

Megan resume her place at the front door and continued looking at the sky.

"You look like you've been to hell and back".

Megan sighed.

Wanda looked around. "Did she come?"

It took a little while before Megan answered. Wanda was willing to wait.

"You just missed her." Megan was surprised at how much strength it took just to answer that question. She turned and walked back to the living room leaving Wanda to close the front door.

Wanda turned to see Mrs. Templeton now standing at the curb straining her neck to look inside. She waved, closed and locked the door on the gawking woman. By the time she walked into the living room Megan was curled into a fetal position on the loveseat. Wanda sat down and gently pulled her sister's feet onto her lap.

"If what happened here is as bad as you look right now, then I only have one question. Was it worth it?"

Megan spoke very softly. "She said she's sorry for what she did to herself."

Wanda frowned. "What does that mean?"

Megan turned and pushed her body up so that her back rested against the arm of the loveseat. She looked at her sister.

Wanda was two years younger and slightly taller and curvier than Megan. She'd recently dyed her short, natural hair auburn which highlighted her soft dark brown complexion nicely.

The only two children born to their parents, through many fights, tears, laughter, marriages (one each) and children (two each) the sisters remained very close. Megan thought Wanda was beautiful and had a picture-perfect life but then again, everyone seemed to have a picture-perfect life compared to hers.

Megan cried softly. The mascara and eyeliner mixed with her tears looked like tracks of dark mud running down her cheeks. "She said she has to go home to nothing," Megan said answering her sister's question. "But I still have Jim."

"Oh," Wanda slowly nodded, "I see."

"Really? Well I don't."

Wanda looked at Megan who was now staring at the ceiling. Her heart broke for her older sister. "Megan, I'm your sister and you know I've got your back. With prayer, God's word says He's …"

Megan snatched her feet off her sister's lap. "No God Wanda. Not now."

"If not now, then when?" Wanda asked softly.

"Both of them ruined my life, my husband and his little 'thing' on the side. So help me I'm going to get them back if it's the last thing I do."

"Stop talking like that."

Megan stood and paced. She went from weak and weepy to frantic and frenetic in a matter of seconds.

"I've been talking to this crack head that sits on the corner by my job. I've been telling him how God can change his life for the better." She stopped pacing. "For $100 he'll kill both of them. For $150 he'll keep his mouth shut and do the jail time too." Megan ran into the kitchen and snatched her car keys off the counter. "I wonder if he's out there now?"

Wanda ran to her sister and, before Megan could react, snatched the keys from her hand. "I said stop talking like that and sit down."

The frenzy stopped as abruptly as it began. Megan shrugged, "I guess you're right. Besides, where am I going in my bare feet?" Slowly she walked back into the living room and plopped down onto the recliner. Her hands caressed the armrests.

"Both of them sat here today." She looked at Wanda and nodded. "It's true. Jim sat here earlier. Stephanie later. Both of them. In this chair. His butt. Her butt," she paused, "now my butt."

Fresh tears filled her eyes. "How could he do this to me Wanda? I'm a good wife. A good mother to our children. I don't deserve this. I don't."

Wanda knelt on the floor in front of Megan and placed her hands on her sister's knees. "I know it's hard for you to believe right now and I understand why you don't want to hear about God, but He's the only One I know that can help you right now. I promise Sis, if you turn this pain over to God He will…"

Megan exploded, almost kicking her sister. "SHUT UP ABOUT GOD!" She pushed Wanda away and stood.

The frenzy was back. "What did He do? He didn't keep His side of the bargain." She paced back and forth like a roaring, caged lion. "I kept myself. I was a virgin when I got married. I went to church every Sunday of my life, even when we were on vacation. I taught my kids about God. I never, ever cheated on my husband. I helped that man succeed. Everything he is today he owes to me. AND WHAT DOES HE DO? WHAT DOES HE DO? AND IN MY BED? IN OUR BED?"

She stopped yelling, stopped pacing and faced her sister. Through clenched teeth she spat out, "Don't you dare tell me anything about God."
~Silence~

Suddenly, Megan snatched the phone off of the charger.

Wanda threw her hands up in frustration. "What are you going to do now?"

"I'm going to call and cuss her out like I should've when she was here." She began dialing then stopped. "Isn't this something? I've memorized this heifer's number."

Wanda snatched the phone out of her hand.

Megan looked at her sister. "I didn't invite you here. In fact, I distinctly remember telling you not to come. So feel free to leave – like right now."

Still holding the phone Wanda replied, "I'm not going anywhere Megan. You're angry and hurting. I think you're angry enough to hurt yourself."

"Hurt myself?" She laughed. "Oh, I can guarantee that's something you need not worry about. I'm homicidal, not suicidal." She looked at her sister again. "Leave Wanda."

"No." Wanda placed the phone back on the charger.

Megan's eyes drifted toward the wedding picture hanging on the wall. The same one Stephanie looked at earlier. She walked toward it and stood on her tiptoes to gently stroke the thick polished mahogany wood frame. "Look at us Wanda. What are people going to say? To our church, our families, to everyone, we were the model family for twenty years." She crumbled to the floor sobbing. Wanda knelt and cradled her sister in her arms.

Megan continued through her tears. "Women use to tell me how blessed I was. How I had a good husband. A wonderful family. They envied me. Wanted to be me. Now that image is ruined. My entire life is ruined. Why me Wanda? Why me?"

Wanda hugged her sister tight as tears glistened in her own eyes. "I don't know why these things happen Mimi."

Megan pushed her away and stood.

Too much nervous energy, Wanda thought as she watched her sister walk the floor again.

"He always said I criticized him too much but that was just my way of encouraging him to do better."

Wiping her nose with the back of her hand she continued, "He often called me Self-Righteous Megan. Said I was going to float up to heaven because, in my own eyes, I never did anything wrong." She stopped and looked at the picture again. "He said I never apologized. Never accepted anyone else's apology …" her voice trailed off as she looked at the recliner.

"Both of them sat in that chair today. Just hours apart. Makes me wonder what else they did in that chair."

Wanda pleaded, "Sis. Please. Don't."

"NO! NO! NO! I am not to blame. I will not blame myself. This is not my fault. This is all on him and her. Him and her. Him and …"

Grabbing the back of the chair she flipped it so that the seat was now facing the floor. Repeatedly, she kicked and punched the chair. "I hate both of them. I wish they'd both die. Drop dead right now. I hate them. I hate them. I hate them."

Wanda crept behind her sister and, wrapping her arms around Megan's waist, jerked her away from the chair. Megan resisted causing both of them to fall on the floor.

"Megan! Stop and listen to me." Wanda straddled Megan, pinning her to the floor. Both were breathing heavily.

"You don't understand Wanda" Megan cried, "your husband would never do this to you."

Wanda rolled off Megan and onto her back. That explosion of emotion took a lot out of both of them.

Released, Megan curled into a ball on the floor.

Wanda spoke breathlessly. "I understand more than you know Sis."

Megan looked at Wanda.

"Just because I haven't told you about certain things in my life does not mean it's been all sweetness. There have been some very sour moments."

"Are you saying…?"

Wanda interrupted, "No, this situation hasn't happened to me but the feelings, the strong negative emotions, feeling no longer secure in your place and the fear and insecurities that in itself creates, I have experienced all of it. That is why I'm saying I understand what you are going through. I understand the feelings. It is also exactly why I know that if you don't turn this over to God…"

Megan sat up shaking her head.

Wanda sat up too. "Stop with the negativity Megan. It is and will always be about God."

Both women glared at each other.

Wanda continued, "And if you don't find the strength somewhere deep down inside to turn this over to the Lord, it will take root and become bitterness to your very soul."

Megan rolled her eyes.

Wanda pressed forward, her voice rising in a desperate attempt to get through to her sister. "In an effort to make him and her pay, you will end up being the one paying emotionally, spiritually, mentally and maybe even physically for the rest of your life. And that payment, my dear sister, is way too steep for anyone to make."

Megan hugged her knees to her chest. "So Miss I'm-such-a-holy-Christian, what should I do?"

Instead of hearing the sarcasm, Wanda heard her sister's pain and it filled her heart with compassion. "You should forget about him and forget about her for the moment."

Megan started to protest but Wanda held up her hand. "Just hear me out. Take one minute – sixty seconds to ask God to help you through this. Ask Him to remove the hatred."

Megan looked at her sister, smiled and quietly responded, "What if I don't want the hatred removed?"

Wanda's heart raced. "Stop with the smiling and talking all quiet like that because I'm beginning to think you really are crazy. Since when did you start wanting to hate? We were not raised like that."

"We were not raised like what? Mom put up with Dad's shenanigans for years before he decided to stop cheating. Notice I said when HE decided – she had no say in his decision. Sounds like wife-hood 101 to me. You know that 'just-be-quiet-and-take-it-darling-cause-one-day-he'll-calm-down-then-he'll-be-all-yours' stupid class older women teach the younger ones. Especially old women in the church. Shoot! I wish I would. I mean, how can he possibly be 'all mine' when he's given most of himself away to every whore in town?"

"Really?" Wanda asked. "He had one indiscretion and suddenly it's every whore in town? Now you're really talking nonsense and I don't want to hear nonsense."

"Don't you sound cute. One indiscretion. Call a spade a spade boo. He screwed another woman. At least that's what he confessed to. How do I know it's only been one woman? I mean, that's what he said but how can I believe a liar. And nonsense? You're calling what I'm saying nonsense? Sounds like you passed those old lady classes with an A and more for extra credit," Richelle responded sarcastically.

"We were talking about mom and dad." Wanda reminded her which caused Megan to pause. Seeing she wasn't going to respond, Wanda continued. "Megan, all of that happened with Mom and Dad while we were still babies. Besides, Mom forgave him."

"You're right Wanda, she did forgive him. But she had to put up with the ridicule. Her friends knew. Her family knew. The entire neighborhood knew what Dad was doing or had done."

"Megan, Mom and Dad were a couple of kids who married at eighteen years old and yes, trying to navigate in an adult world having just left their parents' homes was tough for them. Very tough. They said those beginning years were hell as they had to learn how to grow up separately and together. It wasn't until almost a decade after their marriage, after the two of us were born, that they finally joined a church and received the counseling needed to get themselves together."

Megan stared at the wedding portrait hanging on the wall. "I vowed that I wouldn't go through anything like that. So, I waited. I was a twenty-five year-old educated, Christian, good woman BEFORE I got married. I married a college educated twenty-seven-year-old, Christian, good man. I thought that by doing the opposite of mom and dad, I was guaranteed a much different life."

"Don't knock their lives Megan. After fifty years of marriage, both of them have said their good days far outweigh their bad ones. The only reason they shared that part of their lives with us was to show that with God all things are possible, including the repair of broken relationships."

"I'm not knocking their lives I just don't want to re-enact it, at least not their early years." Tears formed in her eyes. "But I feel like that's just what I'm doing."

"But you're not Megan. Mom went through so much more than you. She said forgiving Dad wasn't easy but she wanted to keep her family together, so she made a decision to forgive and that decision paid far more dividends than she ever hoped for or imagined."

Megan stared at the wedding picture and whispered. "I hate them so much."

"Mom and Dad?"

"No."

Wanda laughed breaking some of the tension. "Just joking. I know you don't hate Mom and Dad. Mimi, all I'm saying is make a decision. Accept his apology and stay or accept his apology, leave him and move on. Either decision will be better – has to be better – than living like this. You're in so much pain."

Megan continued in that quiet voice, "Forgiveness doesn't happen overnight and you are the one who is crazy if you believe it does. I have a right to feel anyway I want. I was the one who had everything taken away. I'm the victim. I'm the fool."

"You are not a fool but you're sure talking like one." Fear concerning her sister's mental capacity gripped Wanda's heart. She tried to hold Megan's hands but to no avail. She kept them tightly balled into fists with her arms wrapped around her knees.

"You can begin the forgiveness process right now Megan so stop the madness. While you say forgiveness doesn't happen overnight, the root of bitterness begins immediately and that comes directly from the bible."

Megan leaned her chin on her bended knees. "Right now, I really don't care. The way I see it, if bitterness takes root immediately as you say…"

Wanda opened her mouth but Megan stopped her, "…ok, ok, as the bible says, then so be it. I have a right to that too."

Wanda was dumbfounded. "Are you for real Megan? Come on. What about Grandma and Great Uncle Gabe? Uncle Gabe's drug of choice was alcohol. He used it to dull the pain. And Grandma is a lonely, bitter, angry woman who has plowed through five marriages. Her children, grandchildren and great-grandchildren can't stand being around her because all she speaks is negativity. Both Grandma and Uncle Gabe have one thing in common, they vowed to never forgive their father who is dead and long gone yet is still affecting, or should I say infecting their lives. And there are others – countless others we've met along this road called life. They are all miserable. And the people they refuse to forgive? They've moved on with their lives. Is that what you want for yourself? Do you want your entire life, your world, your spiritual, mental and emotional growth - do you want all of that to stop right now? Because that's what is going to happen if you keep this up. Then you won't be any good to yourself, your children or anyone."

Wanda frantically searched her sister's eyes hoping to see a spark of understanding or something. But Megan's eyes remained flat. Almost lifeless. She grabbed her sister's hands and held them tight when Megan tried to remove them. They looked at each other.

"Sis, I love you too much to watch you throw your life away. You are not emotionally built to hold onto this negativity. No one is. You think you're in control but you're not. You're losing – not winning."

Megan yawned.

Wanda released her hands. "Oh, so I'm boring you now? I get it. You win. You're right. You do have a right to hatred and bitterness and whatever else goes with those things. But, do me a favor. Make sure your 'rights' don't 'write' a check your LIFE can't cash."

"Finished?" Megan asked sarcastically.

"Not yet." Wanda responded matching her sarcastic tone. "When you don't forgive, God doesn't hear your prayers so honey, make sure you read the fine print on your rights".

Megan looked at the picture again. Wanda looked too and softened. "I agree with you Megan. An image has been dissolved. But can't you see? Now God wants to rebuild on a real foundation."

"Leave Wanda."

Wanda's heart broke as she watched Megan stand, walk to the front door and open it.

"Leave. Please. I want to be alone."

She looked at Megan who was now leaning against the door staring at the sky. *Déjà vu. This is the same position she was in when I arrived. I don't know if I was able to get through to her.* Wanda never felt so helpless. *God please help her. She's making such a huge mistake. I don't know if she'll come back from this. She's so fragile Lord. Please help her.*

Resigned yet confident the Lord heard her silent prayer, Wanda stood, walked toward the door and gently laid her hand on Megan's cheek. "Call if you need me. Day or night. I'll come right over if …"

"Leave now," Megan interrupted removing Wanda's hand from her face.

Wanda looked at her once more before stepping outside. As she turned to speak again, Megan closed the door in her face. Wanda winced when she heard the lock click into place.

Inside, Megan spoke to herself. "See Wanda, even you pity me. That's why you started crying. I'm such a loser."

Megan leaned her forehead against the front door. At the same time, Wanda laid her hand on the outside of the front door. It was as if Wanda laid her hand on Megan's forehead to pray for her – only they were separated by the door.

Wanda prayed aloud, "Lord please. I beg you. Help my sister." Then she turned and walked to her car.

CHAPTER 4 – DEAR GOD

Megan ran upstairs. Throwing herself across the bed, she pushed her face into the pillow and screamed so long and so hard she nearly passed out. With almost all of her energy gone, slowly she turned onto her back and stared at the ceiling.

"Everything is destroyed."

She got on all fours, crawled to the middle of the bed and sat up straight, not leaning against anything. Her legs were stretched out in front. She looked up.

"What are You doing to me? Do You get off playing games like this with Your children?"

Megan rolled off the bed and began pacing, never stopping her one-sided conversation with God. "I tried it Your way most of my life. I did what the bible told me to do. I did what the leaders told me to do."

She stopped pacing and screamed toward heaven. "I WAS OBEDIENT!"

Megan listened as the last word echoed throughout the bedroom. Quietly she continued speaking to her Lord.

"It's quite clear You don't want me to be happy. If the joy of the Lord is supposed to be my strength, then I'm doomed because I've got no joy, no happiness, no nothing. Nothing but pain and sorrow."

Megan walked to the ivory chaise on the other side of the bedroom and sat. "I thought we had a deal, God. A contract, no a covenant. Isn't that what You call them, covenants?"

Crossing her legs she explained, "See, I thought if I did then You would do and if I didn't do then You wouldn't do. Like, take for instance the scripture, 'delight yourself in the Lord and He will give you the desires of your heart'. HA. That use to be one of my favorites. But now? No offense God but, let's just say You led me to believe if I lived my life Your way – the way You wanted me to live - then everything good would come my way."

She stood. "Oh yes I expected little bumps in the road but doesn't the 23rd psalm say, 'surely goodness and mercy shall follow me all the days of my life'?" Exaggeratedly she looked behind her. "Well, where are they?"

Sitting again, Megan closed her eyes. "This is why a lot of people don't want to have anything to do with You. This is why some people say You don't exist." Opening her eyes, she looked upward. "I'm starting to think they're right."

The last sentence brought about a fresh flow of new tears. "If I can't even rely on You then who? I have nothing. I am - nothing."

Turning she spotted her wedding picture sitting on top of the nightstand. It was an 8X10 replica of the one hanging on the wall downstairs. The frame was heavy, made of beautiful smoked glass. She walked over and picked it up, caressing the frame while her finger traced the smile on her husband's mouth. She smiled as she traced his lips, his hair, his cheeks with her fingers . Though both of them were in the picture, her focus was only on Jim.

"You were so happy. We were so happy." She smiled, "So very, very, very happy."

She looked upward again. "This was the life You promised me or at least, that's what I thought." Hugging the frame close to her body, she closed her eyes. Immediately an image leapt into her imagination…

It was a beautiful Spring Sunday afternoon. Church was over and all of the members filed downstairs to eat lunch in the basement. The older ladies of the church toiled in the kitchen during service to prepare lunch for the fifty members. Fried chicken, macaroni and cheese, collard greens and Kool-Aid were the main menu for years.

Having finished eating, nine-year old Megan, her sister and four of their friends went outside to play Double Dutch. They were used to people staring at them as they jumped rope in their ankle-length black skirts and white long-sleeved blouses, standard choir wear every Sunday during the mid to late 1970s. Somehow, they mastered the art of holding the flapping bottom of those ankle-length skirts so that it wouldn't interfere with the rope.

The image caused Megan to smile as she remembered …

Tammy and Rose turned the rope and sang along with Bethany, Wanda, and Ashley as Megan jumped.

"I'm jumping for Jesus so get it right. He's the only One who guarantees a good life. No pain or sorrow when He is near. My future is bright because He holds me dear."

Megan opened her eyes, walked back to the bed and sat down. While staring at the bedroom wall, the image in her mind changed …

The girls in the class snickered. Even Sis Williams smiled because every week it became Megan's 'mission' to take the class off topic.

"Go ahead."

"It's kind of hard being a virgin when most of the girls in school are not. There's so much pressure to just give in and do it. Right?" she asked looking at the others in the 'all-girls' class as they nodded in agreement.

The Sunday School class was not 'all-girls' due to a separation of the sexes. It was 'all- girls' because there weren't any teenage boys in that church at that time.

Once again Sis Williams smiled. "It may be hard but then again God never said it would be easy. However, He did promise to reward your obedience. Trust me when I say, those other girls are not happy. They are searching for something – something you already have. Dignity. God is the one who gives us that - dignity. A healthy self-esteem. Self-respect.

As we develop our relationship with Him, as we read His word, we learn that our own birth was not an accident. We are so much more than a collection of particles that accidentally formed, collided and spat out the human race. We learn from God's word that we were lovingly fashioned and created by the Almighty Himself for a specific purpose. His word tells us we are royalty and as a result, we are to act like, no, we are to BE royalty. Now, am I right?"

"Yes," the girls responded as one.

Sis Williams smile widened as they high fived each other. "Now, what is our response when a boy says, 'if you love me, you'll have sex with me?"

Megan stood. "I had to say these exact words last week to a boy in my class who asked me if I knew that sex was love. I said if you really love someone then I don't see why sex couldn't wait until after the marriage. I said that I believe the process is, get to know me, develop a relationship, fall in love, get married, THEN have sex. Only it won't be just having sex. I told him it would be making love."

"What did he say after you said that?" Bethany asked surprised that Megan had the guts to say that to a boy.

Megan smiled, "He said, you're the type of girl I would marry because you're special."

Sis Williams responded, "Very good Megan. What that young man said is very true. And guess what, all of you young ladies are very special."

The girls high fived each other again. Sis Williams was very proud.

Eyes still closed, Megan shook her head to clear her mind but suddenly another image appeared.

Twenty-three year old Megan was in her mother's kitchen bouncing around like a rabbit.

"Mom. I can't believe he asked me to marry him. I mean, I know he loves me and I really love him but marriage?" She twirled around holding her left hand in the air showing off her new diamond engagement ring.

"I don't know why you can't believe it," her mom replied, "that young man is not a fool. He has discovered what your father and I have always known, that is that you are a precious, priceless jewel. In this day and age, it is rare to find young women like you and your sister. Both of you fear God and have kept yourselves pure for the man He will give you. Jim wants to make sure nobody snatches you from him. I like a man who sees what he wants and goes after it." She smiled while watching her daughter twirl and dance around the kitchen.

"Stop all of that dancing and sit down for a minute. I need to talk to you."

Megan fell into the chair, put her hands on the table – left over right – and continued staring at her ring. "I hope this isn't about the birds and bees because you and daddy have been telling us about that ever since I could remember."

"And it's a good thing we did because by the time you and your sister were old enough for the boys to start with their tricks, both of you were already wise to them."

Megan laughed. Her mother reached over and gently lifted Megan's chin. "Honey, you kept yourself all these years. You remained pure, a virgin against all odds."

She moved her hand from Megan's chin and placed it on the table. "You were much stronger that I was at your age. Now the truth is, I could blame that on a number of things – my parents didn't teach me the things we taught you and your sister – I became a Christian much later in life – blah, blah, blah. All of that is true but the real reason was because I was a follower. It took a long time before I became a leader. Correction, it took Jesus to raise my self-esteem before I could become a leader."

"You're the best Mom in the world. Everyone should have a mother like you."

Mom laughed, "Well I'm not going to dispute that but still, the truth is, I wasn't what they call a 'good girl' when I was your age." She grabbed both of Megan's hands, surprised at the sudden emotion that overtook her. "That is why I admire you and your sister so much. Both of you are the kind of women I wanted to be but was too weak to be."

Releasing Megan, Mom reached for a napkin, wiped her eyes and blew her nose. "Whew. Child, I don't know where all of that came from."

Reaching for a napkin too, Megan wiped her now damp eyes. "Thanks Mom."

"Let's stop all of this crying and let me finish what I have to say." Mom took a deep breath. "Ok, now where was I? Oh yes, if you don't think God is going to reward you for following His commandments then you, my dear beautiful, intelligent daughter, are craaazzzzyyyy!"

Megan laughed.

"It is the Lord's good pleasure to shower His children with gifts. Not because of who you are, but because of who He is. He is a promise keeper and will keep His promises to you my beautiful daughter. And Jim, well your daddy and I think he's the best of the best and believe me, your father wouldn't settle for anything less for his baby girls. I've often told you that daddy and I got married because I thought I was pregnant. Turned out I wasn't at that time but we went ahead with the wedding. We were in love but not

> equipped to handle the responsibility of marriage. Thank God that for the most part we enjoyed our marriage although we had some rough times, especially in the beginning. But you? Jim asked you to marry him because he loves you. He really does. And he will be a very good husband, father, provider - a very good everything! I can just see it all over him..."

The image dissolved plunging Megan back into her harsh reality. She dropped the picture frame.

"Stop smiling at me," she hissed looking down at the photo. Fury soaked every fiber of her being. She reached for it.

"I hate you. I hate you and that piece of…"

Wildly she threw the frame hitting the full-length mirror. Both shattered and pieces of glass rained down onto the carpet, frightening her. Slowly she walked toward the mirror, knelt down and touched the broken glass.

"Oh dear God," she whispered. "What did I do? What did I do?"

CHAPTER 5 – IS IT ME?

"Mmmm. Shattered. Just like your life."

Startled, Megan turned around and stopped breathing. Standing in the door was a woman who could've been Megan's identical twin. Wearing a black leather corset so tight her bosom bulged out of the plunging neckline, matching tight black leather leggings, thigh high six-inch black pencil heeled pointy boots and tossing her very long, very wild yet very sexy jet-black wavy hair, the woman stood with her arms folded staring at Megan.

Her makeup, though weird, was flawless. Flames in a shiny black lacquer color, leapt from her left cheek to just below her left eye. Her full upper lip was painted in that same shiny black lacquer color. The lower one was frosted white. Her eyelashes were long and fluttered as if some invisible wind was blowing on them. Though the makeup was bizarre, Megan couldn't help but think that standing before her was the sexiest woman she'd ever met in her life.

Still kneeling and wondering why she wasn't running out of the house screaming at the top of her lungs, Megan's eyes followed the woman as she walked toward the mirror and stood over Megan looking down at the shattered pieces of glass.

Suddenly, she began singing in the most horrendous voice known to man. "Memories, light the corners of my mind."

The sound was so repulsive it caused Megan to put her hands over her ears.

"Misty water colored memories, of the way we…."

Feeling physical pain from the singing Megan screamed, "SHUTUP."

The woman smiled revealing a mouth filled with beautiful, even white teeth. "Ahh, she speaks. Good. The anger is good too. Keep it. That's what gives you your self-respect."

That voice, Megan thought, *it sounds just like mine.*

The woman bent down looking directly into Megan's eyes. "You're gonna need that you know – self-respect." Throwing her head back she laughed loud, hard and ugly.

Who is this woman and what is she doing in my bedroom?

"Oh come on now," the woman said. "You know who I am."

Megan gasped and thought, *I didn't ask that question out loud.*

The woman began walking around the bedroom like she owned it, "Negativity."

"Negativity?"

Negativity sat on the bed and crossed her legs in a manner so seductive it made Megan tingle.

If only I could do that and look just as sexy. But, is she me? Dear Lord, am I losing my mind?

"Nope."

"Nope?"

"What are you, a parrot or something?"

Oh sweet Lord, I am losing my mind.

"No, you're not losing your mind. Well, at least not yet." Again, Negativity leaned back and laughed. Somehow her laugh made Megan feel dirty.

This strange woman is reading my mind.

"Strange? Oh come on Megan. Mimi. Stop acting like you don't know me. You and I have had many, many, many chats over many, many, many years."

"What?"

Rolling her eyes Negativity explained, "I'm that negative side of you. You know, the side that feeds you negative thoughts on a constant basis."

Megan's face lost all color.

"Ah, now you get it?"

Slowly Megan nodded.

"Good." Negativity walked to the dresser where she began looking at the items on top of it. "I thought I'd come visit you in the so-called flesh instead of rooting around in that head of yours."

She touched the picture of Megan's children. "We've got some serious stuff to scrutinize and analyze."

Grabbing the photo that fell out of the shattered picture frame, Megan stood, walked toward the chair and sat. She stared straight ahead as if in a trance while addressing Negativity's earlier remark.

"I haven't lost my self-respect. I didn't do anything wrong."

Like something out of a movie in a blink of an eye, Negativity was suddenly standing inches away from Megan. She looked confused. "Are you kidding me? I mean, are you for real?"

Instinctively, Megan tried to turn away but Negativity was so close their noses almost touched.

"You failed." Negativity hit the 'f' on the word 'failed' so hard, saliva flew out of her mouth landing on Megan's cheek.

Megan recoiled in disgust as she wiped it away.

Negativity began dancing and singing, her voice, if possible, sounding worse than before. "Your marriage is a failure. Your marriage is a failure." In a flash, she was kneeling in front of Megan, no longer singing. Her voice took on a menacing tone as she placed the palms of her hands on Megan's thighs.

"And do you want to know the worst part my darling? Soon everyone will know just how big of a failure you really are."

Megan's eyes filled with tears. "This is between me and my husband. No one else will ever know."

Negativity dug her nails into Megan's thighs. "Get a grip, stupid."

"Stop," Megan cried, "you're hurting me."

Negativity raised her hands in mock surprise. "Oh my," she said sarcastically, "I didn't mean to hurt you. Not you. Never you. Besides, there are others already doing that, right?"

Megan quickly turned trying to rub away the pain she still felt from Negativity's nails digging into her thighs.

"Did you say no one will ever know?" Negativity pitied Megan. "My poor little dumb one. Don't you know these things have a way of getting out?"

She stood and paced the room waving her hands like a lawyer speaking to an unseen judge and jury. "Let's review. You told your family so somebody else knows. You went to counseling so somebody else knows. You told your Pastor so again, somebody else knows."

"My family would never betray my confidence. And as for the others, they are professionals. They can't divulge that information."

Negativity stopped pacing and casually leaned her hips against the dresser. "You really are a naïve one, aren't you?" She paused before continuing. "Don't sleep on family. They're the biggest gossips ever. And concerning those professionals, they SHOULD NOT divulge that information. They CAN divulge anything they want. And believe me they do. After all," she began singing a twisted version of Human League's 1986 song titled 'Human', "they're only human of flesh and blood they're made."

Megan's eyes darted nervously from left to right as she realized the truth in Negativity's words. She whimpered, "God will cover me."

"God?" Negativity shrieked. "I thought you would've gotten the memo by now. If God does exist, then He's playing you girl."

Megan's eyes slowly drifted back to the photo in her lap. Negativity walked behind the chair and leaned over to look too.

"Beautiful, huh?"

Megan nodded.

Negativity shifted and suddenly, her face was in the photo. Megan was looking at Jim's body, clad in his tuxedo, but the face was Negativity's - in 3D - talking from the photo. "Beautiful - just like you WERE!"

Before Megan could comprehend what she just saw, Negativity shifted again and was now leaning over the back of Megan's chair. It was as if she never moved. Megan shuddered.

Negativity continued. "Now that other woman, what's her name?" Negativity snapped her fingers as if trying to remember though it was obvious she hadn't forgotten. "Um, oh yes, Stephanie. Now that young piece of sexy is BEE-U-TEE-FULL." Seductively she began running her hands along her own body while describing Stephanie.

"Young. Tight. And oh so right." Though she stopped speaking, her hands continued caressing her own backside.

Megan almost vomited. "STOP!" she screamed. "Please," she begged.

Negativity ignored her. "Yes. Tight and right." She leaned down very close to Megan's ear and taunted, "Just like you use to be. Ah, but those days are now long gone my saggy bottomed friend."

Megan bit her lip as tears flowed down her cheeks.

Negativity stopped feeling herself and smiled. Slowly, gracefully, like an elegant contortionist, she sat on the floor next to Megan's chair crossing her legs in one of those impossible yoga-like positions. She leaned her head against the chair, near Megan's leg. "Well, as they say, you can't roll back time, can you?" She looked up at Megan, "so what's the plan now?"

Megan stared, unseeing. "We will rebuild," she whispered. "Like Wanda said, we can rebuild on a new foundation."

"Rebuild? What the…?" Negativity slapped her knee in frustration. "Oh come on girl. Cut the crap. You know good and well you can't rebuild. What is that anyway – rebuild? Just words darling. Just words."

"Not just words. Action. And it has to begin with me. Wanda said that too. I can be transformed by the renewing of my mind." Megan stood and paced.

Negativity's eyes followed though she remained seated on the floor.

She mimicked Megan, "I can be transformed by the renewing of my mind."

Her voice went back to normal. "Is that the King James version of the bible? Ahh, good old King James. The way he had the bible written, it just made every scripture sound like it is guaranteed to happen just like that." She snapped her fingers on the word 'that'."

"But Megan, you have to use your brain on this one. I mean rebuild? How? I guess that could happen but, all by yourself? I mean, can you do that? Can anyone do that? Rebuild a relationship all by oneself? Doesn't the very definition of relationship involve more than one? So how can only one rebuild? And what about the pain? The humiliation? How are you going to rebuild with all that pain inside of you?"

What about the pain? Megan thought before collapsing mid-stride, in the midst of the shattered glass. *She's right. There's so much pain.*

Smiling, Negativity continued, "That's right darling, don't forget about the pain. To forget the pain is to let him win. That's why he keeps asking you to forgive him, because forgiveness will let him off the hook. Make it seem like nothing ever happened. Like he never hurt you. The only one who will benefit is Jim."

Megan sobbed.

Negativity's voice took on a soothing tone as she stood and slowly began walking toward Megan. "Don't forgive him darling. Hang on to that pain. Make him suffer like he's made you suffer. Look at you. You're still suffering. You will always suffer. You will always carry this pain."

Still on the floor, Megan picked up a large piece of the shattered glass. The edges were sharp and jagged. She studied it closely, feeling the weight, running her finger along the edge.

Overcome with excitement, Negativity silently jumped up and down. She focused on Megan, trying to push her a little more to the dark side. "It really is the only thing left to do. There's no other way. And when Jim discovers your body … oooooooooooo, he is going to be real sorry for the way he treated you."

She continued, gently prodding, "You will have exacted the ultimate revenge on him – guilt - and he will have to live with it until the day he dies. So go ahead. Make Jim suffer. Kill yourself."

Sobbing uncontrollably, Megan placed the sharpest edge of the glass against her throat.

Not forgiving is like you drinking poison hoping it will kill the other person. Instead, you end up killing yourself. The other person goes on living his or her life. Now you tell me, when you withhold your forgiveness, is that your goal?

Megan gasped, "That's my voice. I said those same words when I taught that group of young people at that teen conference last year."

"Uh, oh." Negativity frantically looked around for the source of the voice.

Megan lowered the glass from her throat. Still surprised she whispered, "That was my voice. Those were my words."

Negativity was angry – no, she was livid. She looked at Megan who was still reflecting on the words previously uttered by her – though not really by her.

"Not this one," she said to the unseen source of the voice. "I am not losing this one. You want to do voices, well let's see how you like this."

She opened her mouth slightly. Voices poured forth.

"That's the way I like it baby."

Megan snapped to attention. "That's Jim!"

The voices coming from Negativity's mouth continued, "Nobody can do you like me honey. I make you feel good, right big daddy?"

Megan's heart slammed against her chest. "Is - is that Stephanie's voice?" She shook her head to clear it. "What's going on?"

She looked at Negativity. "Are you …? You're doing this. You're saying those things. Why? Why are you doing this to me?"

Negativity opened her mouth wider. Impossibly wider. It was as if someone flipped a switch and just like that, Negativity's mouth became a 75-inch screen color television broadcasting Jim and Stephanie - in bed - making love - in high definition!

Unable to turn away from the scene, Megan watched intently as hatred began to consume her.

Jim was lying on his back, naked. Stephanie was on top, straddling him. She wore a red laced push up bra and nothing else.

"This is incredible baby," Jim said, his eyes dark with desire.

Stephanie breathed hard, "all for you baby." She thrust herself harder. "This is all for you."

Jim moaned, closed his eyes and climaxed.

Gradually Negativity closed her mouth fading out the last scene of a very sexually satisfied Jim. Though her mouth was now closed and the screen disappeared, Megan continued to stare as if still watching the scene.

"Forget about making him suffer Megan," Negativity's voice was back to that soothing tone. "He doesn't deserve one more second of your time, emotions, thoughts or love. Especially your love." Slowly she walked toward Megan. "End your suffering right now."

She circled the kneeling Megan, "I mean, what have you got to look forward to anyway besides more pain – more betrayal."

Now kneeling beside Megan, Negativity whispered in her ear. "End the pain darling. End the pain now."

Megan was hysterical. "You're right."

"Of course I'm right."

Megan spoke to the air as her misery sunk to an all-time low. "Stephanie is so beautiful. How can I compete with her?"

Negativity jerked her head. "Compete? Um, did you see her? There's no competition. No, it's very clear my dear that you are the biggest loser, only you didn't drop weight – you added tonnage." She laughed at her own joke.

Megan looked at herself again in the shard of glass. "I couldn't bear it if Jim left me for her."

Negativity absently looked at her nails. "It would be very, very embarrassing. We are talking a huge, major, colossal embarrassment beyond belief."

"But that's what - oh dear God, that's what he's going to do. He's going to leave me. And why not? I can't ever be her. Instead, I'll always be…" Megan stopped and looked at her reflection in the shard of glass she was still holding. "Look at me. I can't compete. I just can't."

Slowly, haltingly, as if struggling to choose between life or death, Megan once again placed the sharpest edge of the glass at the base of her throat piercing the skin. A drop of blood appeared.

> Children are a blessing from the Lord. It is up to us to raise and train them up to achieve their God-given purpose. This is our job, not anyone else. It may take a village to raise a child but as far as that child is concerned, dad and mom are the chiefs of that village.

Megan dropped the glass as if it were on fire. "Those are my words again. That's what I taught at the Family Life Retreat two years ago." She looked around. "Why am I hearing my words? My voice? What is going on?"

She stood and backed away from the area. "I can't kill myself. What will happen to my children? They are worth living for." She shivered. "I'm worth living for."

While Megan encouraged herself, Negativity frantically searched the room again looking for the source of the voice.

Megan wrapped her arms around her body and began rocking back and forth while chanting, "I am worth living for. I am worth living for. I am worth living for." She walked to the bed, sat down and continued rocking and chanting.

The voice left Negativity very anxious which was apparent as some of the bravado left her voice when she spoke. "Wh - what about the pain? You- you can't live with all of this pain. You just can't."

Megan stopped rocking. "That which doesn't kill me will make me stronger."

Negativity actually cowered but Megan hadn't noticed however, she did note the slight abatement of that depressed feeling. It was as if someone removed a small load from her back.

Enjoying this new found, though slight lightness in her spirit Megan continued, "Psalm 118:17, I shall not die, but live."

Something sucker punched Negativity in her gut. Bowled over in severe pain, she held her stomach while frantically looking around.

It wasn't Megan, she thought. *I was watching her the entire time. No way she could've punched me. I would've seen it coming. Something is not right here.*

The punch hurt so much it took a few minutes before Negativity could straighten up. Not seeing anything or anyone, but knowing they were not alone, she angrily whispered to the room, "She's mine." She waited for a response but none came. Embolden she turned her focus back to Megan. She took one step toward Megan then, remembering the blow to her stomach, quickly stepped back. Angry and standing flat-footed, arms at her side, she screamed, "JIM MADE LOVE TO ANOTHER

WOMANNNNNN!" Her voice echoed off the walls throughout the room.

Megan collapsed, falling backwards onto the bed.

This time, Negativity took a confident step forward. "When all of this comes out, and believe me it most certainly will, what will everyone think?" Half expecting another punch, she placed her hands on her stomach to shield it.

She waited.

Nothing happened.

Megan slid to the floor, weeping.

Negativity smiled. Reasoning to herself the punch was just a fluke, she boldly knelt then leaned in closer to Megan, so close, her lips practically touched Megan's left ear. "You do remember what you said about the other wives who went through this very same thing, right? They confided in you. Opened their hearts to you. Divulged their deepest, darkest pain to you. And what did you do? Oh, of course you counseled them. Did and said all the correct things to them. Ahh, but behind their backs. Remember what you said behind their backs?"

Megan's eyes rapidly darted left and right. She could feel Negativity's hot breath in her ear.

"Well, just in case you forgot, let me remind you." She spat out the words. "You gossiped about them. Pitied them. Blamed them. Even laughed at all them."

"No I didn't."

Negativity pulled back. "Maybe you're right. In fact, you are right. You didn't do that to ALL of them. But you definitely did it to some of them. Should I name names? Do I really need to name names Megan?"

Too numb and ashamed to speak, Megan closed her eyes and shook her head no.

"Now you tell me, why do you think others will treat you any different?" Negativity paused.

The silence was deafening.

"You can't even answer my questions and you know why? Because you know I'm right. They won't treat you any differently than you did them. Guess what dear? IT'S REAPING TIME."

Megan sobbed from the depths of her soul.

"People won't have any compassion on you. Everything you did to them in secret will be done to you publicly. You will be the laughing stock of your family, your church, your community, the entire world."

Negativity smiled as she watched Megan roll on the floor sobbing. *Just about at the breaking point,* she gleefully thought.

In the midst of her rolling, Megan heard a very small voice say, "Weeping may endure for a night, but joy comes in the morning." She was shocked. In the midst of insurmountable pain, not only did she remember the scripture, she actually spoke those sacred words. That small voice was hers.

As the words flowed from Megan's mouth, an invisible fist hit Negativity with a force so great it knocked her off her feet. Her body was thrown into the far wall, her head absorbing most of the impact. She passed out for a few seconds. Coming to, slowly she shook her head to stop the ringing in her ears. Remembering what just happened she quickly jumped to her feet, looking around the room, fists balled poised for a fight.

~Silence~

She looked at Megan and was momentarily stunned. *Wait! Wasn't she just rolling around on the floor a second ago? When did she get into that kneeling position? Her eyes are closed and her mouth is moving but I can't hear anything. Tell me she's not praying. PLEASE, SOMEBODY TELL ME SHE'S NOT PRAYING.* For the first time in a long time, Negativity was VERY afraid of Megan.

Megan opened her eyes and looked at Negativity. "You're – you're evil." The realization frightened her. "I can see it in your eyes. You're not here to help - you're, you're here to hurt me. But - why?" Still on her knees, she began backing away.

Fear left Negativity. *Ah, now she's the one who is afraid. Good. I've got her on the ropes,* she thought. *Now I'm about to knock her out.*

Negativity opened her mouth. The 75-inch color, high definition television screen was back. The scene was Jim and Stephanie once again making love.

Megan looked at the screen and felt pain. "A minute ago I felt an unexplainable peace come over me but now it's leaving. That peaceful feeling is leaving."

Desperate to get her peace back, Megan tried to reason with Negativity. "I'm tired. I can't go on like this. I can't – I don't want to be miserable anymore." She waved her hand at the screen. "Please make it stop. I don't want to see it." She closed her eyes. "I don't want to hear it." She covered her ears with her hands.

"Tell me I'm better than your wife." Stephanie said to Jim on the screen. "Hey!" Jim abruptly pushed Stephanie off of him. "My wife is off limits."

Megan's eyes shot opened. Her hands fell to her side.

Negativity frantically tried to close her mouth. She pushed at her chin and even covered her mouth trying to silence the words, but she couldn't. Her eyes darted back and forth anxiously. It's like something is holding my mouth open, she realized. She tried to run out of the room but her entire body felt as though it was frozen in place. She couldn't move. She couldn't close her mouth. All she could do was flail her arms like some sort of crazy antenna. Megan's only focus was on the screen.

Jim sat up. "What am I doing?"

Negativity tried to cover the large screen with her arms but to no avail – in fact, the more she moved the more the volume increased.

Megan, transfixed by the scene playing out on the screen, clearly saw the panic in Stephanie's eyes as she tried to regain her position back on top of Jim while coaxing him to lie back down.

"Forget what I said. Come on baby. No need to stop now." She cupped his face. "Just lay back down."

Jim moved Stephanie away with one sweep of his arm. "I can't do this Stephanie." He looked at her. She was kneeling on the bed wearing only her bra. The panic in her eyes was replaced with tears.

Negativity wildly waved her arms.

"This isn't right. How could I be so stupid? I'm sorry Stephanie." Jim said. "It never should've gone this far." He buried his face in his hands. "Dear God, what am I doing?" He looked back at Stephanie. "I don't love you Stephanie. I love my wife. I love the life we've made and - I'm a fool for trashing all of that for - for this."

He leaned down to pick up his pants from the floor then looked toward heaven. "This is not the kind of man I want to be. God, please forgive me."

He turned back to Stephanie. "Please forgive me for doing this to you. Get dressed and leave. Somehow, someway, I've got to make this right."

"Noooooo!" Megan screamed. Still on her knees, she fell forward, her face buried in the carpet. "He told me he said those exact words to her but I didn't believe him. She told me the same thing. I called both of them liars. Every time he apologized I called him a liar. Oh God, how could I have been so stupid?" she cried while repeatedly banging her fists against the floor, "How could I have been so - oh God, help me."

Megan wallowed in self-pity for a few minutes before realizing the only sound in the room was her own voice. She looked at Negativity, whose arms were still flailing however Megan focused on something else. The image on the screen was frozen. It was Jim's face. His eyes were looking out from the screen. He was looking directly at her. Megan stood and reached out as if to caress his face though she was not close enough to touch the screen.

"He looks so sad," she whispered to herself.

Oh crap, Negativity thought. Her eyes roamed the room. *Ok, ok. I give up.* She hoped her unseen assailant could read her thoughts since she was not in control of her own mouth. *She's yours. Let me go. I know when I'm whipped.* Worn out she stopped flailing her arms and stood, unmoving, her mouth still open. She looked at Megan and her eyes became slits.

You weak piece of trash. Mere garbage. Can you hear my thoughts like you use too? If you can, then listen and hear me good. If you think you can get rid of me that easily, think again. We've been together too many years. Do you think you can really throw me aside just because you want to? What are you going to replace me with? Joy?

Peace? Puhleaze! You wouldn't know any of those things if they bit you. It's been you and me for too long darling. Nothing will ever change that. In fact, I promise you, it will only get worse. Why don't you just die? Huh? Just die. Die. Die. Die.

Oblivious to Negativity's mental tantrum, Megan whispered, "A wise woman builds her house, but a foolish woman tears it down with her …" she raised her hands and looked at them, "… her own hands." She dropped her hands to her side. "I have been such a fool."

A sound emanated from the screen startling both of them.

I didn't do that. Negativity thought.

As if someone pressed rewind, the film went all the way back to the beginning. The image of Jim and Stephanie, in the throes of passion, was now back on the screen - frozen.

Megan continued to stare at the image as the old negative feelings began vying for their place back into her heart, their home for such a long time.

Negativity felt slight movement in the corners of her mouth. I moved. *Ha. This means she's coming back to my way of thinking. That's right Megan, come back to your only true friend - me.*

As if someone pressed play, the show began again – this time in slow motion - but before a word was spoken or a groan uttered, Megan yelled, "I FORGIVE YOU JIM."

Negativity's mouth clamped shut and try as she might, she couldn't open it. *What is going on?*

Megan closed her eyes as she spoke to herself, "I do. I really do forgive you Jim. I really do."

An unattached hand appeared out of nowhere holding a needle threaded with very fine yet very strong wire. Negativity watched in panic as it came closer to her lips.

The hand hovered near the bottom right corner of her mouth briefly before it began sewing her lips together with the wire. She moaned in pain as the needle passed first through her lower lip and then her upper lip, repeating the same process over and over again. After each pass, the hand pulled the wire tighter eliciting more groans from Negativity. When her mouth was sewn completely shut, the hand, remaining wire and needle disappeared.

Megan fell to her knees in prayer.

Negativity fell to her knees in pain.

Megan, eyes still closed and unaware of everything that happened to Negativity just seconds ago, softly prayed, "Lord Jesus, can you please forgive someone like me?"

Negativity heard something on the floor. She looked down. What the …? A long very heavy chain with huge links hit the floor hard near Negativity's knees. Her eyes were wide with fear as she stared at it. *Where did that come from?*

Megan heard and saw nothing as she continued praying. "I've been so wrong for so long."

It's moving! Negativity thought she was going to hyperventilate. The chain came to life and in a snake like motion, began moving toward her left side. With her knees frozen to the floor, all she could do was swing her head to the left while following its movement. It stopped behind her feet. Negativity's neck hurt as she strained to keep an eye on the chain. Briefly she turned forward to rest her neck then quickly turned back. The chain remained near her feet – unmoving.

"I've been exacting payment from Jim for his crime against me but I've committed so many crimes against You Lord - crimes for which You've already paid the price - for me."

As Megan prayed, the chain began wrapping itself around Negativity's ankles. She tried to scream but her mouth was sewn shut. She tried to stand but couldn't move.

She tried scooting away on her knees but again, she could not move. There she knelt with her lips sewn together as the chains bound her feet.

Megan continued praying but became very angry with herself. "Who am I to think I'm owed something? I've been so self-righteous."

An unseen force pulled hard on the chain now wrapped around her ankles, causing Negativity to fall prostrate, her face crashing to the floor. She groaned loudly but the sound was muffled. Lifting her head, she tried to will Megan to follow her commands. "Shut up," she screamed but it sounded more like, "mmmm-mmm."

Megan didn't hear anything – not when Negativity fell, not her groans, not her moans nor her muffled sounds. "I don't know how You could stand me. Why would You die for me? I'm filthy. My thoughts," she hung her head in shame, "oh God, my thoughts. They are so - vile." She looked toward heaven.

"I was filled with so much pride. I couldn't see it before. I can't believe I didn't see it because now it's so clear to me. Oh Lord, I'm not worthy of Your forgiveness but please, I ask like the psalmist, that You purge me and I shall be clean. Wash me and I shall be whiter than snow." She smiled as the tears ran down her face. "And You and I both know that's going to take a whole lot of washing." She laughed at her own joke. For the first time in a long time, she really laughed. It felt good.

As Megan continued laughing and praising the Lord she felt as though weights of various sizes were literally being flung off her body and into an unseen abyss.

This was very different from what Negativity was experiencing. As Megan spoke to the Lord, the same unseen force roughly pulled Negativity's hands behind her back and clamped them with invisible handcuffs leaving her palms facing up. She tried in vain to move them. She tried rolling her body from side to side to break free of the leg chains. She tried with all her might but was unable to move any part of her body except her head.

"Jesus, please forgive me." Megan felt as if sunshine had burst forth in her soul. She had that warm, bright 'no-matter-what-the-circumstance-everything-will-be-alright' feeling. "Thank you, Lord. Thank you, Jesus." Her heart was dancing, flying, soaring.
 "Thank you so much. This really is that peace that passes all understanding. Nothing has changed - yet I have changed - so everything has changed."

She opened her eyes and found herself looking at a fallen and weak Negativity.

She sees me. Negativity strained her neck as she tried to look up and maintain eye contact with Megan. *Don't let me go Megan. You need me. I will help you gain respect. Honor. Love. The love you are entitled too. Just don't let me go. We, you and I, must never forget the wrong perpetrated against us. WE MUST NEVER FORGET!*

Though Negativity's words were unspoken, Megan heard them. Grabbing her head, she rocked back and forth in an effort to shake the negative thoughts from it.

"My thought life. Lord please, save me from my own thoughts. Forgive me and save me from the negative thoughts that roam around in my mind. I'll do my part, I'll stay in Your word and in prayer. I'll keep my mind on positive things. Good things. I'll try to find the beauty in everyone and in everything. That's the only way to renew my mind. And that is what I must do if I am to survive mentally – I must renew my mind."

Negativity heard the chains rattle. Frantically, she turned her head trying to see what was going on. The portion of the chains that were not wrapped around her ankles hung suspended about six feet in the air, just above her back. The chains swayed slightly causing that rattling sound again. She looked back at Megan screaming loud the only thought left in her head, *don't let me go!*

Megan folded her hands in prayer. "Lord."

"Umpf." Negativity felt a sharp pain as the full weight of the chain dropped onto her back.

"I want to do the right thing. I don't like this heaviness. Un-forgiveness has left me in a very dark place," Megan prayed.

From the center of her back, the chain slowly began snaking down her right side. Negativity felt it crawl beneath her stomach and over to her left side. After it made a full revolution, it remained underneath her body.

"Help me. Teach me how to forgive my husband. Teach me how to forgive - period."

The chain began moving again making another loop around her left side, only this time, it didn't stop but kept making full revolutions around her entire body.

"It's not easy Lord, but it's necessary. I don't like existing. I want to live life and even that more abundantly."

Levitating, Negativity's body was now floating and spinning in the air as the chain wrapped itself around her entire body, from head to toe.

"For years – decades – I've lived my life as judge and jury, finding anyone and everyone guilty who dared hurt me," Megan cried. "But how many people have I hurt - intentionally and unintentionally? Some forgave me. I didn't even ask, no, I WOULDN'T ask for their forgiveness - but they gave it anyway. Even then, I wouldn't accept it."

Negativity hit the floor with a thud. Wrapped in chains from head to toe, the only thing visible were her eyes.

Megan looked into those eyes. "How many times, intentionally and unintentionally have I hurt You, dear Lord." She swallowed hard. "Forgive us our trespasses," she whispered, "as we forgive those who trespass against us. That's scripture. That is written in Your holy word.

How could I think I was in a relationship with You when Your word made it clear that every night when I got on my knees and asked You to forgive my sins, I received exactly what I gave to others?"

A tear filled Negativity's right eye. The left one twitched.

"Wanda was right. If I don't forgive then I can't expect You to forgive me." Megan screamed again, "I FORGIVE YOU JIM!"

Negativity fainted.

Megan fell out of her kneeling pose and into in a fetal position. "I forgive you honey. I forgive you. I forgive you."

Again, Negativity's body levitated then began spinning, slowly at first then at an impossibly fast speed.

Megan laughed with real joy, "It feels so good to say those words Lord. So - freeing. I forgive you Jim and I forgive everyone who has ever hurt me throughout my lifetime. I forgive everyone."

Negativity exploded in mid-air. Like pieces of an unassembled puzzle, parts of her body and the chain hung briefly suspended in mid-air - then disappeared.

"I forgive everyone. I forgive everyone. I forgive everyone." Megan chanted those words over and over again.

CHAPTER 6 – A HAPPY ENDING?

Jim stayed at the office as long as he could. It was 7:00pm. If he waited any later to leave, he would either be subjected to the cold shoulder or an inquisition from Megan.

He pulled into the driveway an hour later. The house was completely dark except for the light in their bedroom. Instead of exiting the car, he sat back in his seat.

"She's in the bedroom." He unhappily smiled. "Just a few years ago one light in the bedroom and the rest of the house dark meant the kids were fed, washed and in bed, and I was about to be greeted by my beautiful wife in a new sexy negligee she'd purchased just for me."

Slowly he shook his head. "Not tonight. Not anymore. Not ever."

He leaned forward and looked up at the light again. "Gotta man up. Can't stay away. Gotta go in."

Slowly he got out of the car, opened the back door to retrieve his coat and briefcase, closed both doors and walked toward his house. He put his key in the front door and stopped.

Leaning his head against it Jim prayed, "God, I know this is all my fault. I know I brought this all on myself and I know I've got a lot of work to do to make this right but…" he paused as emotion filled his voice, "… can I please get one night of peace? Is that too much to ask? I mean, I know I deserve everything she's throwing at me, but I don't think I can take much more. It's getting …" He stopped. Taking a deep breath, he opened the front door steeling himself – ready for another series of assaults from Megan.

Slowly walking upstairs carrying his briefcase and coat, his feet felt like lead. He wouldn't allow himself to think. He just kept walking. As he reached the top he heard her crying. Falling against the stair rail he fought for composure.

I can't do this anymore. Tears rolled down his face as thoughts rolled around in his mind. *I can't stand to hear her in this much pain. Pain that I caused.*

Unable to walk, he sat down onto the top step. Dropping everything, he buried his face in his hands. "Knowing that I hurt her … She's my wife for God's sake. I'm supposed to love her. Protect her. Cherish her. Not hurt her. I never, ever meant to hurt her. Not like this. Not like this."

Jim sobbed. "I'm not the man I want to be. I'm … She doesn't deserve this … I can't … Oh God."

He sat on that step crying for some time, all the while listening to Megan's sobs. Finally, physically and mentally exhausted, he stood, wiped his face with his hands and began walking toward his bedroom, thinking.

I'll leave. That's what she wants. That's what she said this morning so I'll leave. And I'll give her the house, the kids, all the money I have and anything else she wants. I'll give her all that I have and if she needs more, I'll get it for her. Someway. Somehow. It's the least I can do. I won't fight her on anything. If that's what it takes to end her pain - if that's what it takes to make her happy again, then I'll do it. I'll do whatever she wants.

He reached his bedroom, took a deep breath then walked inside. The first thing he saw was Megan lying on top of shattered glass that littered the rug. Fearing the worse he ran to her and knelt down. A piece of glass pierced his pants and cut into his knee but he didn't care.

"Can I hold you? Please?" Even as he asked, he reached out and pulled her close. The tears began again.

"I am so sorry Mimi." He stroked her hair. "Baby, please, please listen to me." As she turned toward him, Jim saw blood on her throat. In horror he looked at the glass on the floor.

"Baby! You're bleeding! Did … did you try to …" Unable to bear the thought of her trying to commit suicide because of his deeds, he leaned back and screamed, "NOOOOOOOO!"

Understanding his fear, Megan tried to talk. "Jim," was all she was able to get out before he stopped her.

"Megan, I – I … oh dear God. Megan. Please. I don't want you to suffer like this. I'm so sorry baby. I'm so sorry. Please forgive me. Please forgive me." He placed his head on hers and sobbed.

Megan realized just how much pain he had endured too. Gently, she touched his face. "I forgive you Jim." She smiled, "can you forgive me?"

Caught off guard, Jim tried to comprehend the words coming from Megan's mouth.

"I said I forgive you honey and I hope you can find it in your heart to forgive me ... please?"

Jim's brain kicked into overdrive as he tried to process her words. "You forgive ... Can I forgive ... I ... I'm confused."

Megan pulled away so she could sit up and speak to him face to face.

"I need to know that you forgive me for making all of this so hard. I sat in judgment over you and ended up putting our entire household in an emotional prison."

She wiped a tear from his cheek. "I went through a lot today. A whole lot. Had some harsh conversations with three women today, including myself." She placed her hands on both of his cheeks. "I. Was. Wrong."

Jim was shocked.

"So, I'm asking again, I forgive you Jim. And I'm asking you again, can you forgive me?"

Jim couldn't get his thoughts together. He entered the room prepared to leave in order to make her happy and now, here she was asking for his forgiveness.

Am I dreaming? Gently, he removed her hands from his face and slowly stood, never breaking eye contact.

Now Megan was confused. *Is he going too ...his face ... his eyes ... he looks so serious.*

Afraid she silently pleaded with God. *Lord, please, no more confessions. Don't let him confess anything else to me. Please? Not now. I mean, I'm learning how to forgive but please, have mercy on me. I don't know if I could survive another confession. God? Please?*

Jim cleared his throat. "Can I forgive you? Is that what you're asking me?" Clearly in shock he repeated the words. "Can I forgive you?"

Jim leaned down and scooped her up in his arms. Laughing, he spun around causing Megan's legs to swing in the air. Megan, though stunned, laughed too.

Jim stopped moving. The room grew very quiet as he intently looked into Megan's eyes.

Megan smiled. She saw love and gratitude reflected back to her.

"Yes. Yes baby. Megan, I love you so much. I promise I won't ever hurt you like this again. Not ever." His tears splashed onto her face mixing with her own.

"I love you Jim." She was barely able to get the words out. "I love you and me and our family. I love all of us too much to carry this heavy load of anger, bitterness and grief."

She held his face. "We - you and I - will live and not die. This marriage will live and not die. It will be stronger. Our family will be stronger. And the two of us will become – scratch that, we ARE one – once again."

Jim's shoulders shook as he wept. "I love you so much Megan. And I'm so sorry."

She buried her head in his chest. He buried his head in her hair.

If someone took a picture, it would look as if they were one - as they blended into each other.

*Look out for Stephanie's story
coming soon.*

TOPICS FOR DISCUSSION

Which is more important, forgiving, being forgiven or both? Why?

Does that one good reason exist as to why a person should not be forgiven?

The longer you don't forgive someone, the harder it is to let it go. What is the first step that a person should take to forgive after holding onto it for such a long time?

Is un-forgiveness genetic or learned? How is it different from abused people abusing or offspring of drug addicts abusing drugs?

Do you know someone who has benefited from not forgiving someone? Explain.

Do you know someone who has been negatively affected by not forgiving someone? Explain.

Should forgiveness be based on someone asking for forgiveness or accepting your forgiveness?

For example: if you ask for forgiveness and someone says no – now what?

If you forgive someone but they don't acknowledge that they did anything wrong – now what?

Crystal's love for storytelling came from her mother, who spent countless hours telling stories to her children as they sat rapt in attention.

Crystal's talents were made public when she wrote, directed and performed her one-woman skit titled 'Harriet Tubman – I came back to say hi'. After seeing this performance, she was offered an opportunity to write and direct plays for the teen ministry of her church which soon led to writing and directing full scale plays for all ages.

"Reading is my enjoyment.

Storytelling is my passion.

Writing is my life.

Family is MY EVERYTHING."

Follow Crystal to stay in the know of upcoming projects:

www.crystalclearstories.com

crystalclearstories@gmail.com

facebook@crystalclearstories